The Life Cycle

An Educational Children's Story and Metaphysical Explanation of Before,

During, and After the Life of a Human Being on This Planet

The Life Cycle

RICH NISBET

Book Writing Maestros
631 4th Ave unit # 4006
Brooklyn, NY 11232.

Editing – Madeline Maas
Cover and Illustrations - KidsBook Art LLC
Dedication – Excerpt from the song "We'll Meet Again" by Rich Nisbet

First Edition July 2025

ISBN *******************

Book Writing Maestros

CONTENTS

THE STORY 1

IMPORTANT NOTE TO PARENTS AND EDUCATORS 32

EPILOGUE 40

REFERENCES 42

Dedicated to my son

Mick Reed Nisbet

(1995-2023)

We'll meet again
If we believe what we can't see
You'll always be with me

We'll meet again
That part of us that never dies
Son, it's not the end

We'll meet again

ABOUT THE AUTHOR

Rich Nisbet is a versatile professional known for his roles as a musician, counselor, life coach, end-of-life coach, author and podcaster. With a passion for inspiring personal growth and resilience, Rich blends his artistic talents with insightful coaching to help individuals navigate challenges and achieve their goals. As the host of the *It's The Question* podcast, and his interactive website, *Above It All 360*, he shares thought-provoking conversations and strategies for overcoming life's obstacles while maintaining a positive mindset.

During the Covid restrictions, Rich developed self-coaching programs that anyone can do at home. Programs like; *360 Power Surge*, *Life After Loss*, and *Metaphysical Exploration*, each of which provide elevated, life-changing results.

Whether through his music, coaching sessions, or engaging podcast episodes, Rich is dedicated to empowering others to live authentically and rise above adversity and the human condition.

Email: rich@richnisbet.com
Website: richnisbet.com

Books:

- <u>This is Not the End Beautiful Friend</u> – *Steps to Help someone at the End-of-Life Maintain Peace and Dignity While Providing Guidance & Reassurance to Everyone Else*
- <u>This Lifetime</u> – *An Autobiography About Us All*
- <u>The Life Cycle</u> – *An Educational Children's Story and Metaphysical Explanation of Before, During, and After the Life of a Human Being on This Planet*

The Story

The Magic Air

Where all the animals
and humans live

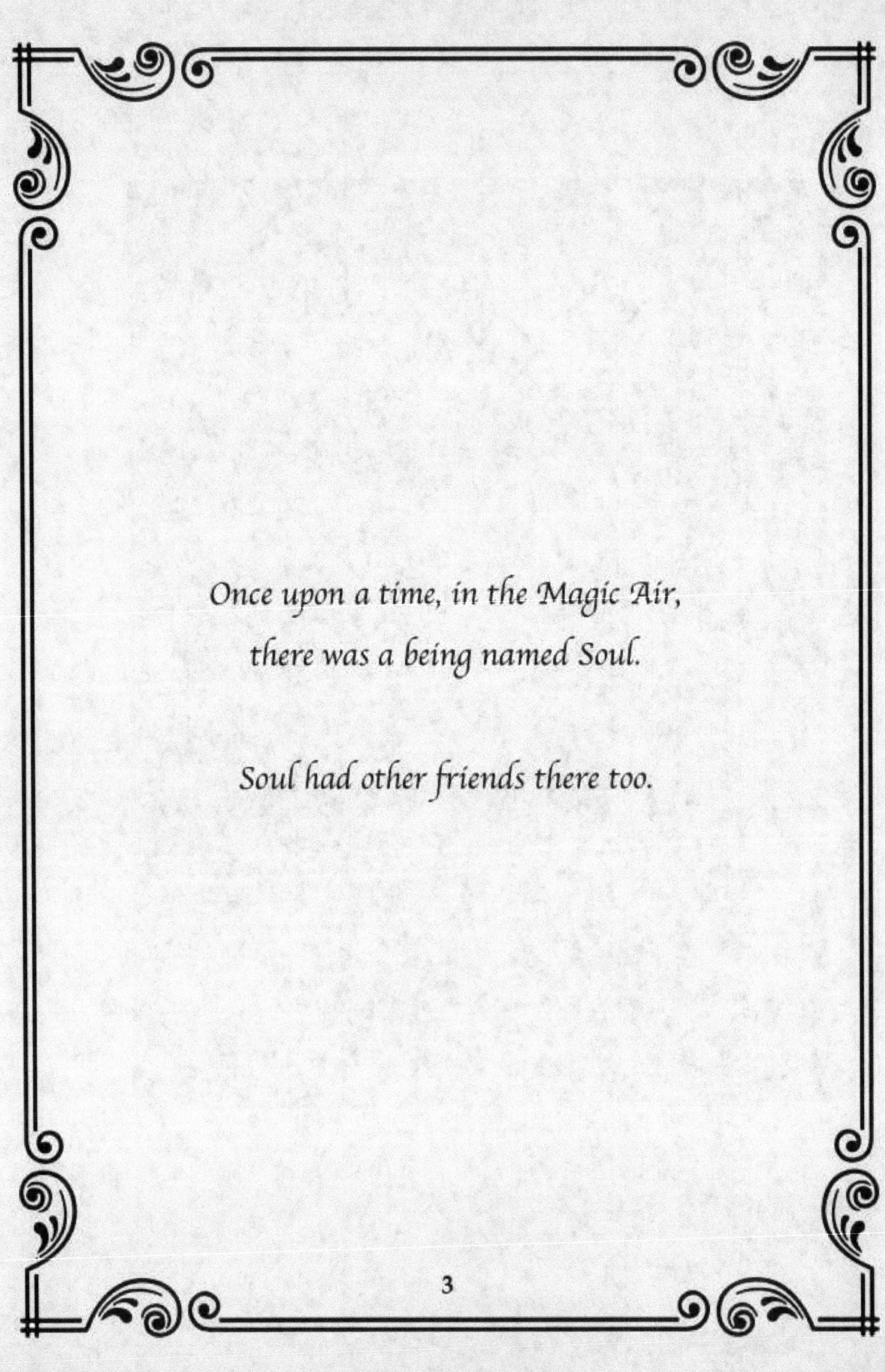

Once upon a time, in the Magic Air,

there was a being named Soul.

Soul had other friends there too.

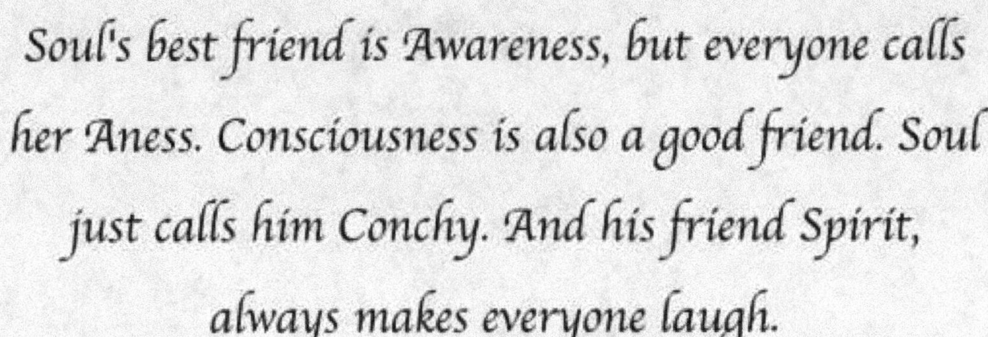

Soul's best friend is Awareness, but everyone calls her Aness. Consciousness is also a good friend. Soul just calls him Conchy. And his friend Spirit, always makes everyone laugh.

One day Soul told his friends he wanted to learn what it would be like to run in the grass, play with toys, and eat birthday cake.

Conchy smiled and said, "But Soul, you don't have any legs to run with!" Aness leaned over and whispered, "And you know Soul, you're also gonna need some hands and arms if you want to play with toys." "Yeah Soul! How you gonna eat cake when you don't even have a real mouth?", Spirit excitedly blurted out.

Everybody laughed and laughed.

Finally, when everyone settled down, Aness flowed all her love and explained: "Soul, if you really desire to learn how to run in grass, play with toys, and eat birthday cake, you'll need a human body to do all that."

So, Soul decided to go find a body he could be with.

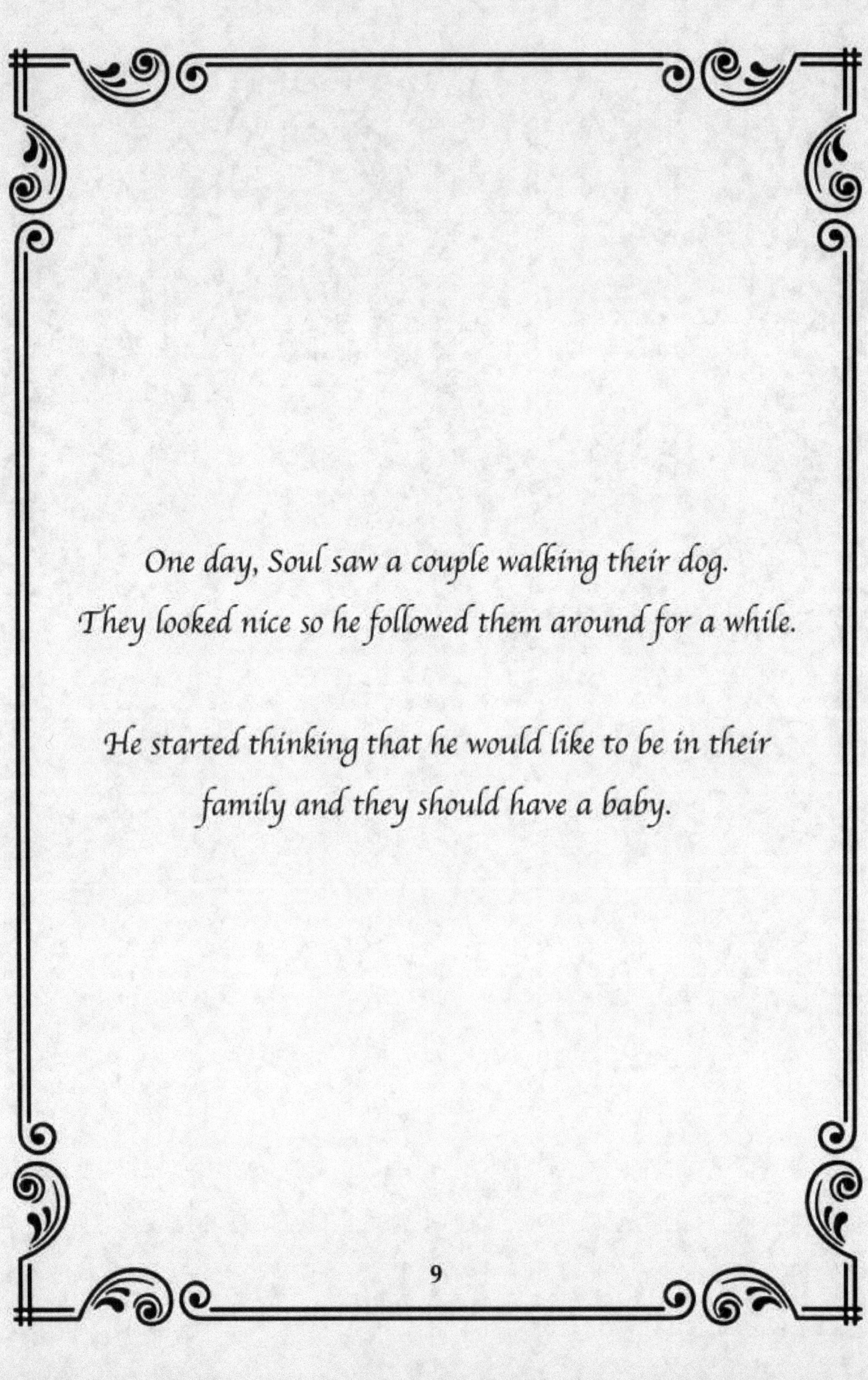

One day, Soul saw a couple walking their dog.
They looked nice so he followed them around for a while.

He started thinking that he would like to be in their
family and they should have a baby.

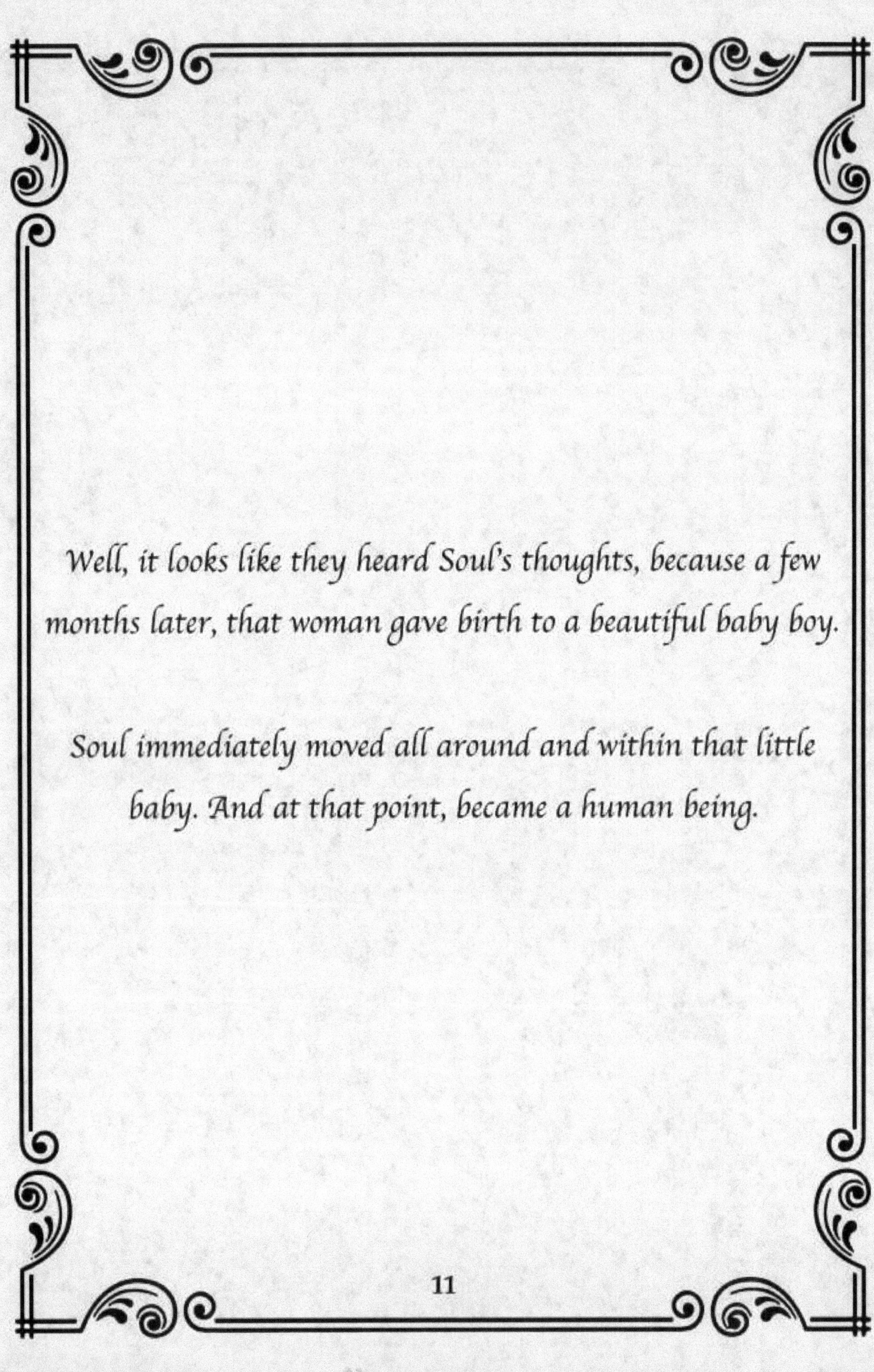

Well, it looks like they heard Soul's thoughts, because a few months later, that woman gave birth to a beautiful baby boy.

Soul immediately moved all around and within that little baby. And at that point, became a human being.

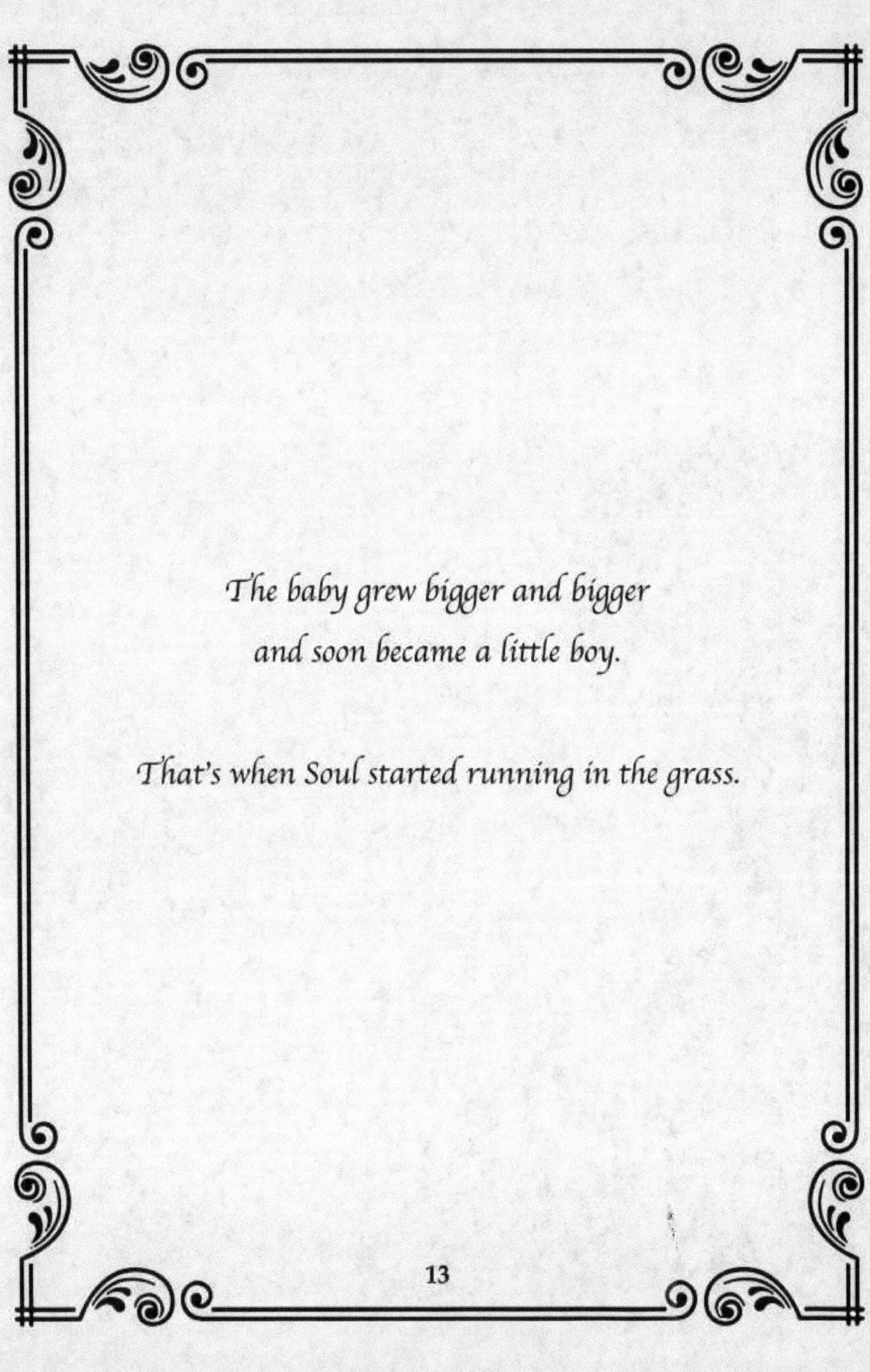

The baby grew bigger and bigger
and soon became a little boy.

That's when Soul started running in the grass.

And playing with toys.

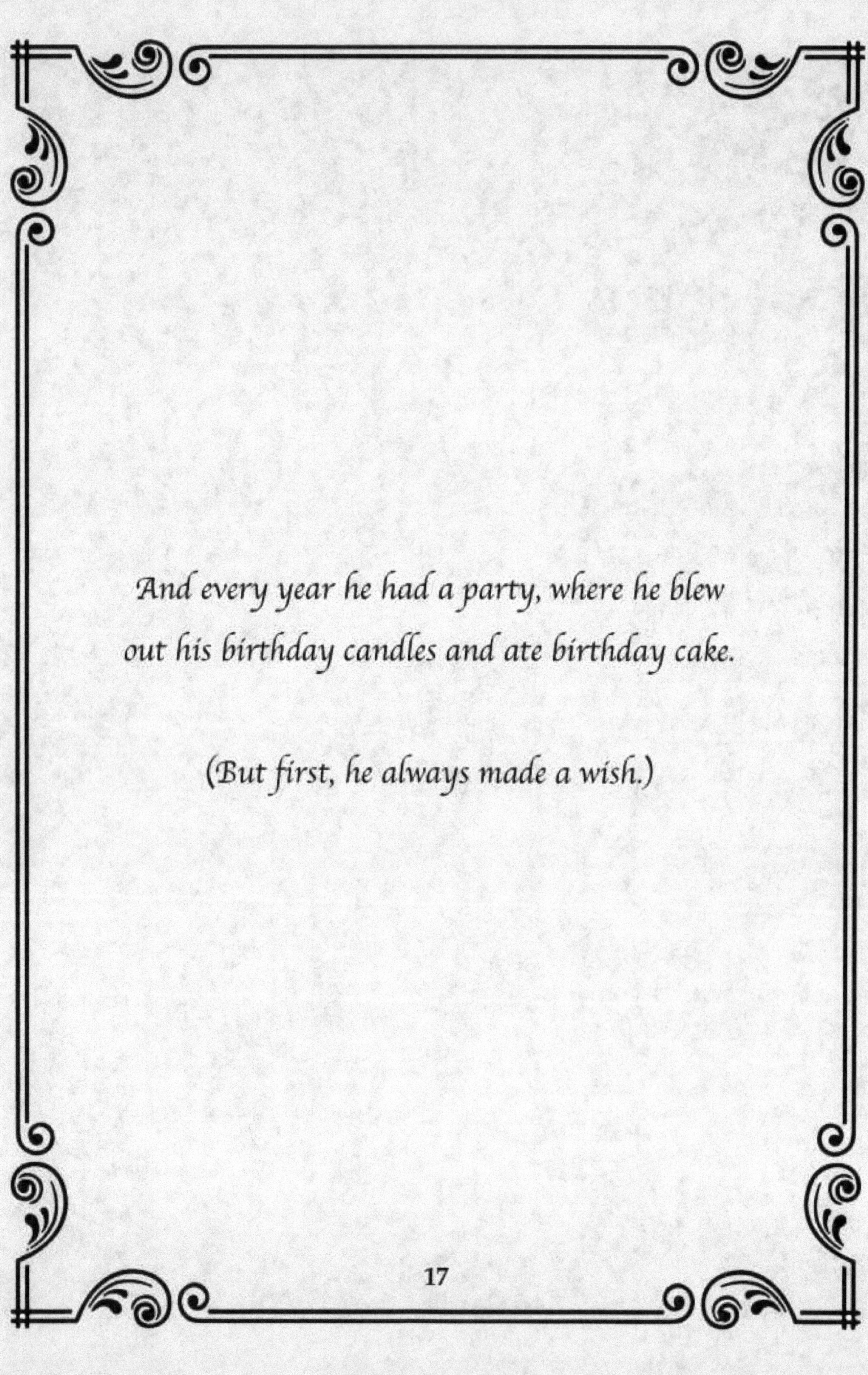

And every year he had a party, where he blew
out his birthday candles and ate birthday cake.

(But first, he always made a wish.)

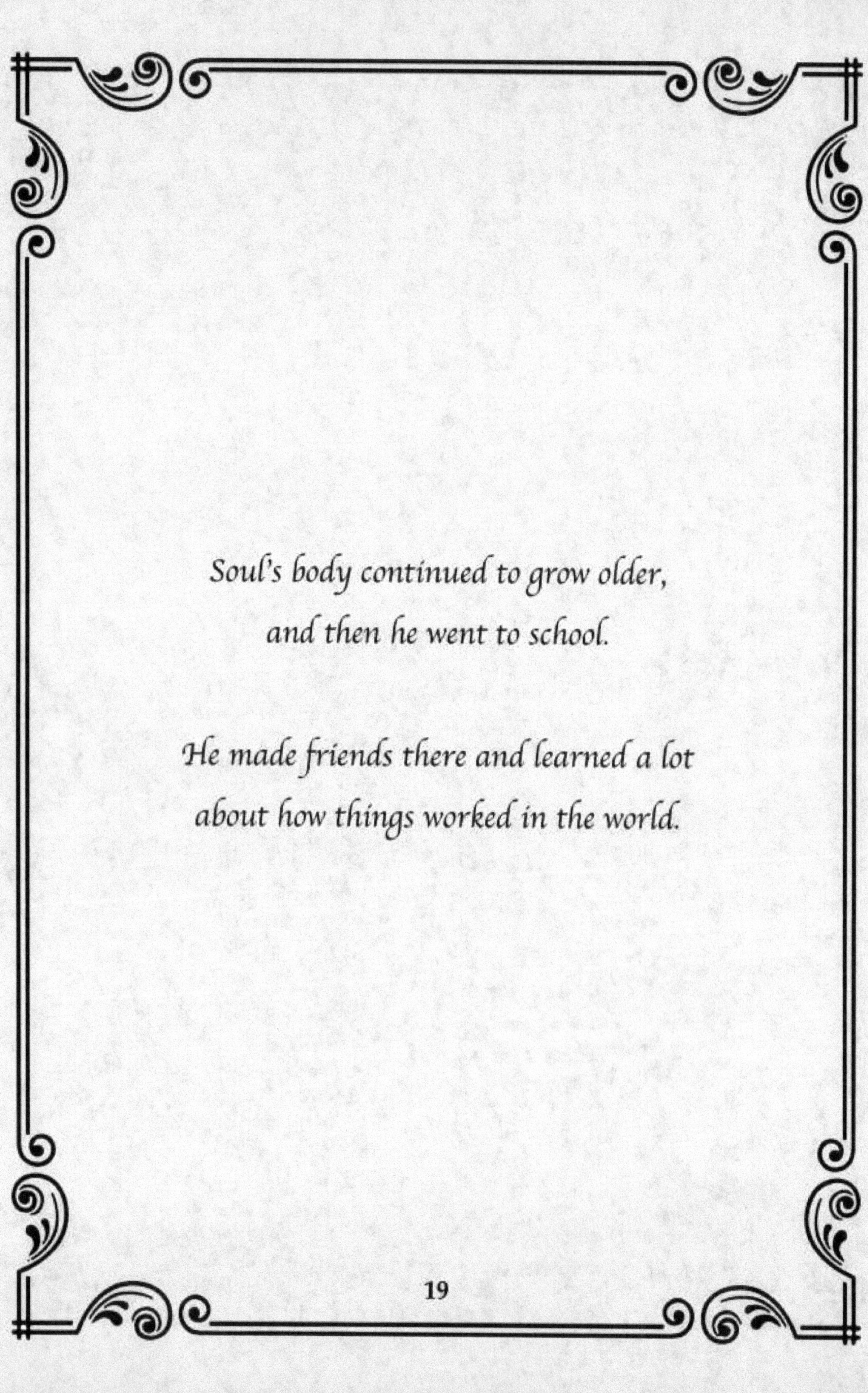

Soul's body continued to grow older,
and then he went to school.

He made friends there and learned a lot
about how things worked in the world.

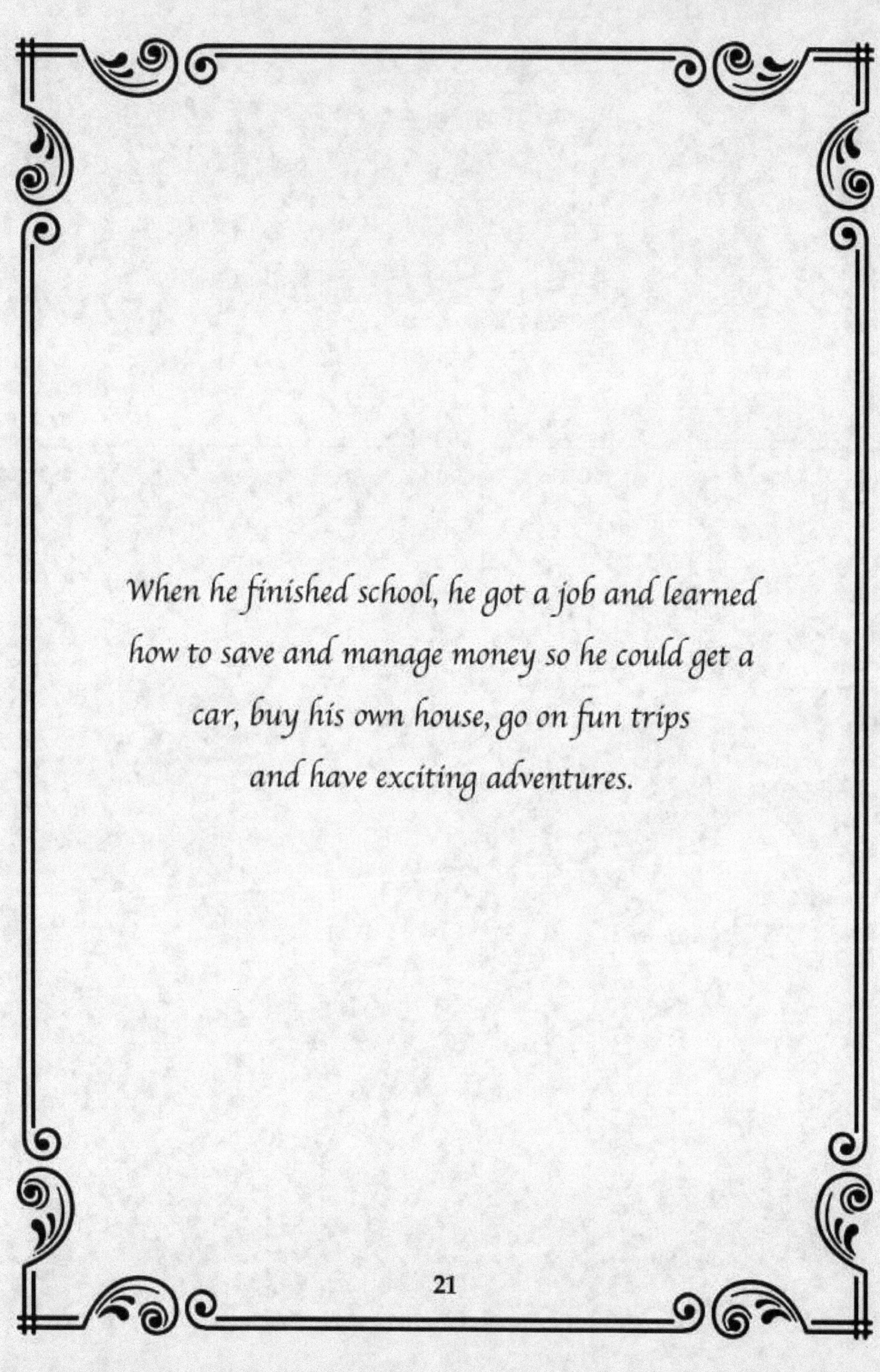

When he finished school, he got a job and learned

how to save and manage money so he could get a

car, buy his own house, go on fun trips

and have exciting adventures.

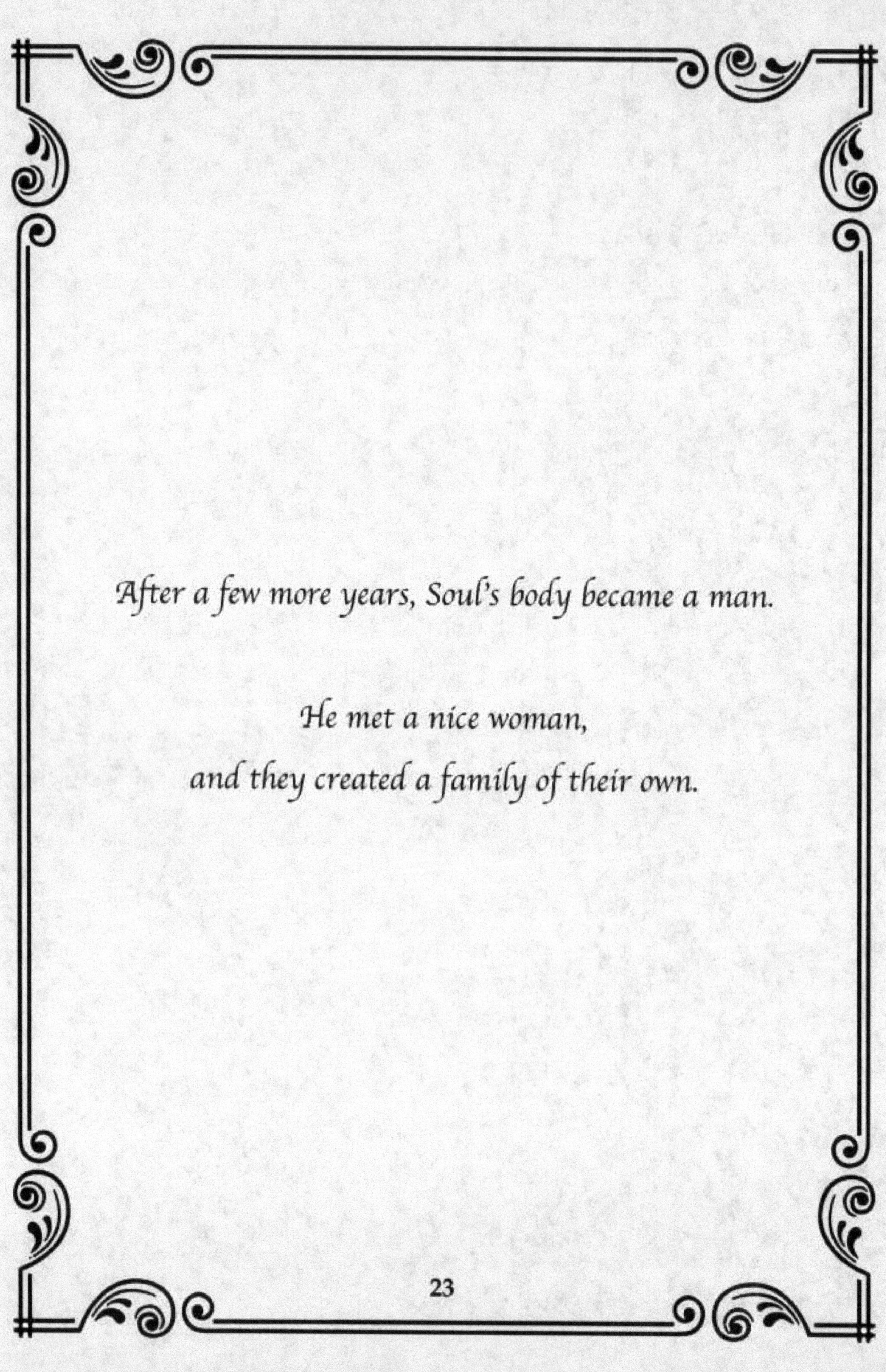

After a few more years, Soul's body became a man.

He met a nice woman,
and they created a family of their own.

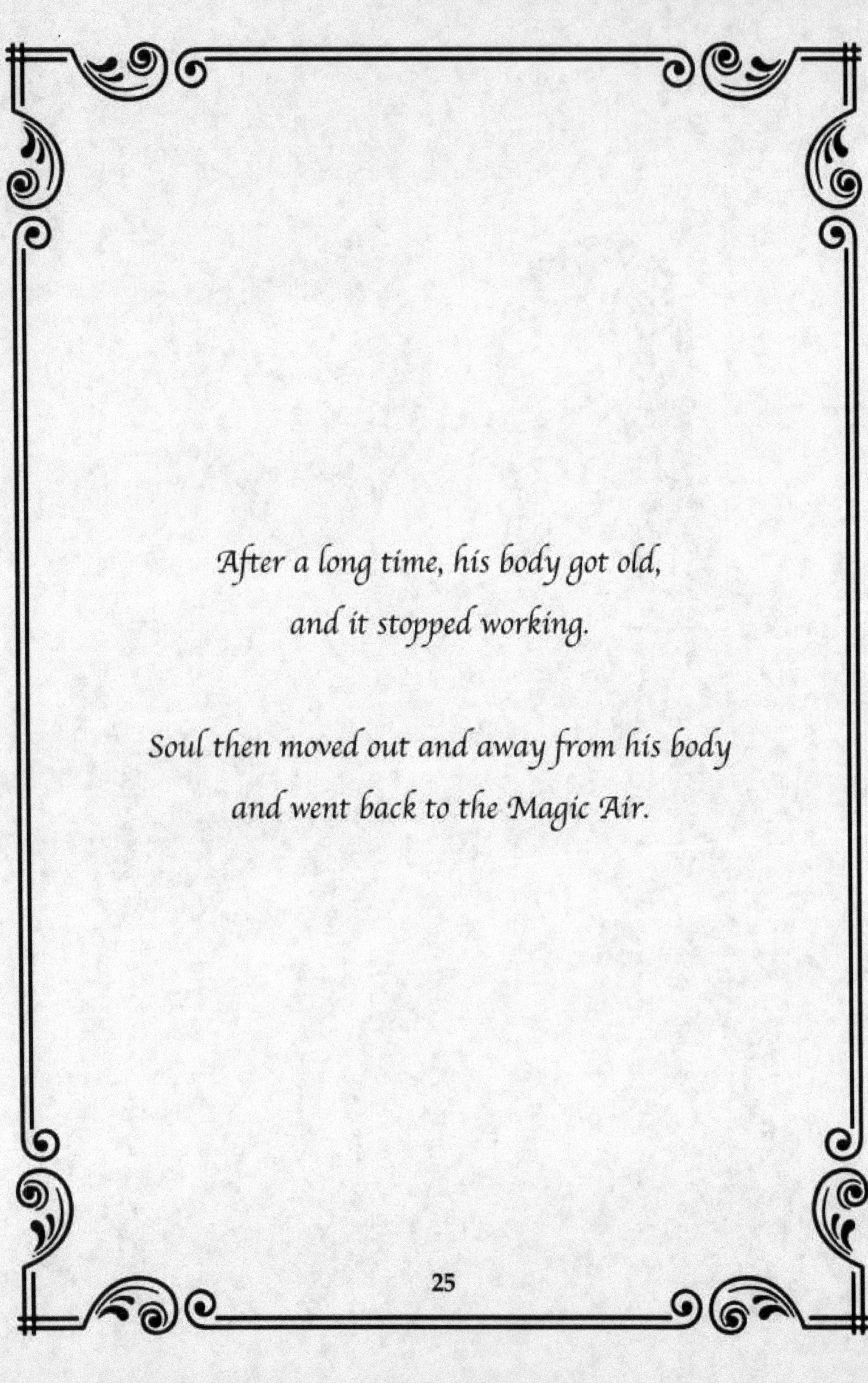

After a long time, his body got old,
and it stopped working.

Soul then moved out and away from his body
and went back to the Magic Air.

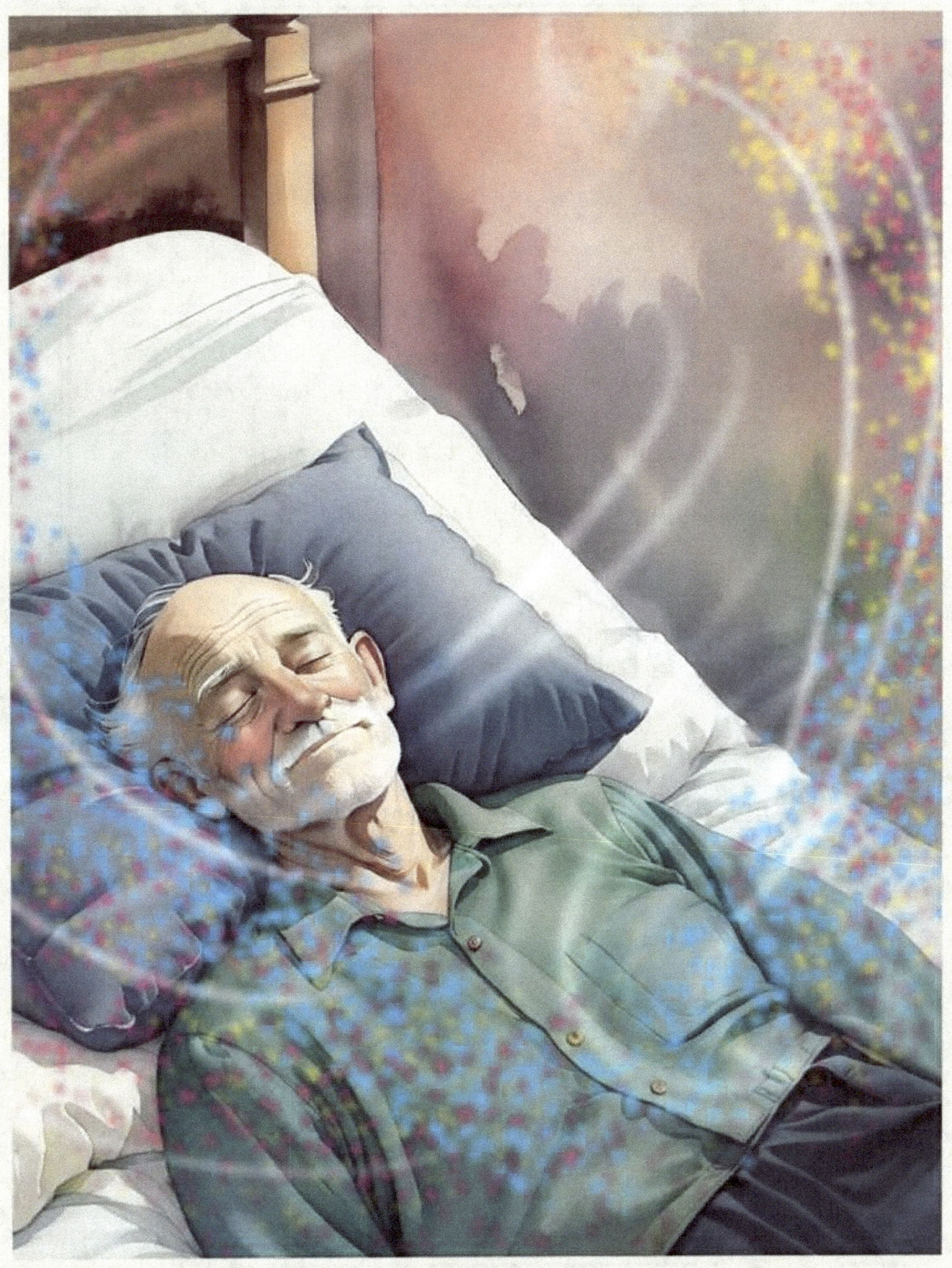

He told Aness, Conchy and Spirit all the exciting
stories and adventures he'd experienced, and
everything he learned while he was a human being.

And he still watches over his family
and will always love them.

Soul continues to learn and create new adventures.

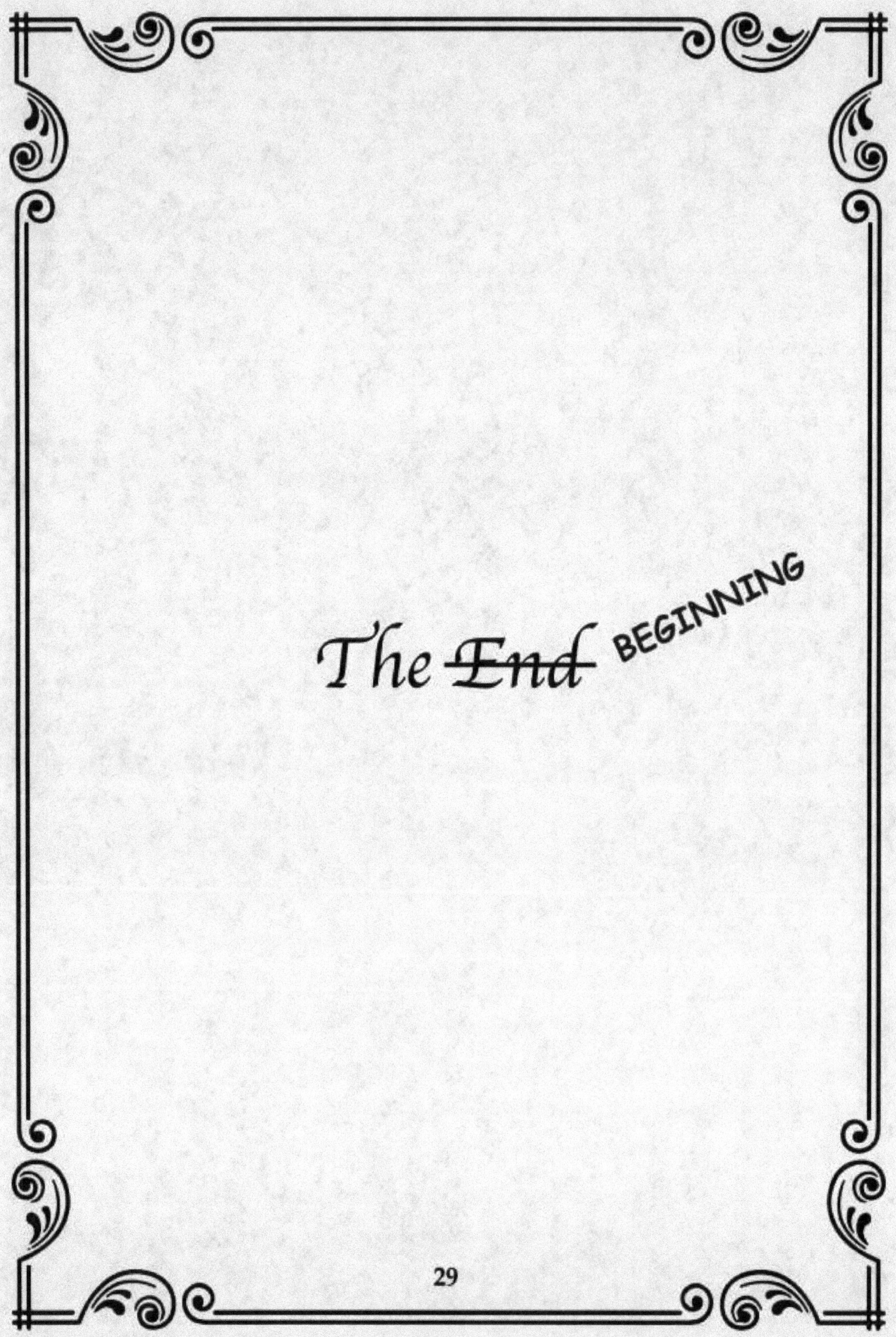

The End BEGINNING

IMPORTANT NOTE TO PARENTS AND EDUCATORS

In December of 2024, I received a phone call from an associate of mine who asked for my advice on what to tell a 3 ½-year-old daughter regarding her recently deceased grandfather.

And that got me thinking.

When a loved one has died, we generally tell our kids statements like:

- Grandpa went to Heaven.
- Grandpa is now in a better place.
- Grandpa has reunited with Grandma.
- Grandpa is now watching over us.
- Grandpa passed away.

Even the term "passed away" insinuates that the person has now moved to a different place other than the location of their deceased body. It's implied and assumed that something left the body and is now somewhere else. Sometimes it is explained that it's Grandpa's "soul" that is now elsewhere.

But, if grandpa's soul left his body, that means at some point the soul would have had to enter that body at an earlier time. Right?

Think about it…

You can't go out of something that you never went into.

You cannot walk out the door of your house if you had never gone into your house to begin with.

You can't leave a job that you did not, at first, get hired into.

You can't break up with a lover if you had never entered that relationship.

Oxford Languages defines the term "cycle" as: A series of events that are regularly repeated in the same order.

The life cycle that occurs for every human being on this planet has the appearance of Birth-Life-Death.

Our typical explanations of what happens at death, only tell a part of the story and part of the life cycle. Children are instinctively going to know that something is "off" with what you're telling them. They will always wonder, have questions, and possibly distrust you and that version of what you're describing.

This book explains the whole story and it is best that your child learn about this entire life cycle before someone passes away. It will be much easier on them when that time comes.

Then comes the question, *"What is the soul?"*

Well, let's see if a simple exercise can help make that concept more real:

1. Touch your right leg.
2. Now, touch your left arm.
3. Now, touch your awareness.

You can't.

When you say, *"I am happy"* or *"I am sad"* or *"I was late for work"*, the "I" that is experiencing, being aware, and conscious of those emotions and situations is You. You are the awareness. You are the consciousness. You are the soul.

Our bodies are physical.

Bodies are born, they live, and then they die. Physical means: "Energy existing and changing throughout space, measured by a medium called linear time".

The soul is *metaphysical*.

Meta, in this sense, means "beyond". So, anything metaphysical is: "Beyond energy, space, and time".

Therefore, the soul cannot be defined in physical terms because it is not physical. It is something else.

Other descriptions used for this non-physical essence are consciousness, awareness, spirit, atman, quantum mind, free will, the observer, the witness, and others.

There is overwhelming evidence we are not our physical bodies and that we ARE a metaphysical consciousness, timeless and deathless. We don't die. Our bodies do, but we don't.

You don't have a spirit; You ARE a spirit. You don't have a soul; you ARE a soul. You possess a house, a car, a body, and a brain. You are not your car, your house, your body, or your brain.

If you say, "Grandpa's soul went to Heaven", you're missing a fundamental aspect to the entire life cycle. Grandpa is a soul. He doesn't have one. "Grandpa is watching over us and his body went into the ground", is a much more accurate description of death.

This distinction is subtle but extremely powerful when you can start applying it in your life.

The story in this book has nothing to do with religion or the concept of God, Yahweh, Allah, Jesus, Buddha or any other terms designating a Creator. Catholics, Buddhists, Christians, Hindus, Jews, Islamic, Spiritualists, and even some Atheists should be able to embrace these concepts without betraying their beliefs.

Questions about where the soul comes from, or who created the soul, go into the realm of religious faith or belief. The story in this book doesn't intrude on those ideas and only acknowledges that there is a soul and that it is a separate entity from the body.

So, when does the soul merge with the body? Well, you can look it up. There are quite a few schools of thought about this. Some think that this meet-up happens at conception. Scientists talk about witnessing a "spark of life" that is visible right when the sperm and egg connect. Some think it happens around the fourth month of pregnancy. I know of one mystic philosophy that claims that the soul is present seven days before conception. Others say that this transition happens at birth, and some have claimed to have witnessed this nuance occurring just as the infant is being born.

I have also been told stories from women who said that when they were pregnant, they experienced all sorts of strange phenomena. Some explained that they were woken in the middle of the night because all these souls were in their bedroom, noisily "fighting" over who would claim that soon-to-be-born baby body. One woman even told me that she received communications as to what name to give her baby!

And regarding those at the end-of-life, two individuals confided in me that when they were present during the death of a loved one, they physically felt and perceived the soul departing from that body and room.

It has been stated that the goal of a child is to grow up.

William Arthur Ward is quoted as saying, "The adventure of life is to learn" and of course, learning is a large part of the process of growing up. The main character in this book wants to learn and experience what it is like doing things a human can do.

Emphasizing the idea that it is desirable and exciting to learn about life aligns with a child's basic purpose. Kids are extremely "tuned-in" to the metaphysical side of life, including magic, imagination, previous lives, and other realms, so this story of a soul wanting to learn and explore new things will always ring-true with children.

The soul, in its innate state, has no actual identity, so this story applies to any human being. Versions of this book could be adapted to fit the gender and race of any child.

Now, why is this story and information so extremely valuable to children and to the parents or teachers who are responsible for raising and/or educating them? What are the implications? Why is it important for your child to know the truth of the life cycle and to know who and what they actually are?

If you possess aspirations for your child to be independent, morally grounded, capable, self-reliant, and happy, while at the same time exercising kindness, honesty, empathy, and respect for others, then then the concepts of this story will help them on that road.

There are tens of thousands of reports throughout the world that have shown evidence of children, predominately between the ages of two and six, who have uttered statements along the lines of the following:

- Children have stated that they chose the family they are now in with statements like: *"I picked you as my mommy"*. (Instagram - @michael.love444)
- Children have said to their parents that they used to be a deceased family member: *"I was your daddy before… when we lived in that house with the big tree that had a crack in it."* They have sometimes relayed detailed locations, situations, and nicknames that they had never been exposed to in this lifetime.
- Children have claimed that they were "talking" to a deceased relative, giving descriptions and details that were 100% accurate. *"Grandpa visits me sometimes."*
- Children have told their parents who they were in previous lifetimes with details, names and circumstances that turned out to be accurate. There are even accounts where children described how they died in their last life and who had killed them, which upon investigation in this current lifetime, the crime was finally solved, and the murderer apprehended by law enforcement. (Dr. Jim B. Tucker – University of Virginia)
- Children have mentioned to their parents' statements indicating that they could "see" (perceive) disembodied souls or spirits. *"There is a man in that back room, and we don't like to play in there"*. (S. Patterson – Michigan)

Recent scientific studies of the human brain indicate that one of its primary functions is to filter out wavelengths, frequencies, thoughts, and concepts that do not directly aid in basic, human survival. Like how a radio filters out all AM/FM frequencies except for the one you have chosen. This allows us to function day to day without our senses becoming overwhelmed.

There are millions of people that have had a "Near Death Experience" (NDE).
This is where a person has technically died, including a total cessation of brain
function, but eventually returned to life. They have reported that when their
body was dead, they had entered a beautiful realm where they could perceive
colors, sounds, emotions, feelings, abilities, beings and concepts that they had
never experienced before when their body and brain were fully functioning.
(Dr. Bruce Greyson – University of Virginia)

The fact that a young person's brain is not yet fully developed may be the
reason so many children are perceiving, open to, and freely communicating
about some of these awarenesses occurring in, as this story refers to, "The
Magic Air".

In science, this is the metaphysical realm physicists call "The Field".

This also may be a be a factor in explaining the savant, autistic genius and child
prodigy. These individuals' brains are apparently not functioning as normal
and so they are able to tap into this realm which is not being hidden, reduced or
filtered out. And so, provides them with access to some amazing,
out-of-the-ordinary perceptions and abilities.

So, parents and teachers, please, please, please, if your child is trying to relay
some of the occurrences listed above, let them tell you about it and listen
without judgement. They may have a better handle on what is going on than
you do, and a supportive attitude on your part will not shut them down and
will help to validate their experiences. You'll allow them to feel safe, which can
help foster trust in you and in their own perceptions and intuitions.

Based on the factors and realities implied in this simple children's story, the
following points could be discussed with your child as they grow and continue
to negotiate the human condition. This knowledge can help them maintain their
integrity and minimize the typical fears, doubts and mysteries of life:

- You don't die. Your body eventually will, but you won't.
- There is a beautiful, metaphysical realm, called in this story "The Magic
  Air". This realm is always present, but it's not readily evident because
  our brains only let us perceive a small sliver. However, there are certain
  activities that we can involve ourselves in that will often "open a portal"
  which allows us to start perceiving and experiencing this magic realm:
  art, creativity, music, writing, nature, meditation, philosophical
  processes, hiking, and many types of outdoor activities on land, air, and
  water, often give us glimpses into this incredible universe of beauty and
  ability.

- There are thousands of stories of people who have received signs and communications from deceased loved ones. Understanding the true nature of the Life Cycle makes us much more likely to perceive, recognize and acknowledge communications or signs from those that have passed on.
- Telepathy, intuition, out-of-body experiences, remote viewing, lucid dreams, and innate knowingness are the types of abilities that exist in the metaphysical realm.
- You, as consciousness, are not part of the linear time stream and so you do not age. Your body does but you don't.
- You are the same you (consciousness) before birth, during life, and after body death.
- Everything physical goes through constant change. You, as consciousness, are the only unchanging constant throughout the life of your body.
- You, as consciousness, are not physical and cannot be harmed, become a victim or suffer, except by your own considerations, decisions and opinions.

In closing, I really want to thank and validate you as a parent, not only for purchasing this book, but also that you care enough about your child to introduce them to the story and ideas contained within these pages. Concepts that may not be mainstream at this point in history.

In my 40+ years as a counselor, coach and end-of-life guide, I have experienced, heard stories from others, and witnessed all the different aspects and phenomena that have been touched on in this book. I have also seen the very positive and encouraging effects this information has had on children.

If we circle back to the original question that inspired this book, the following explanation is a simple version of what you might say to your child, based on this children's story:

"Honey, sit down here. I want to let you know about your grandfather. You know that grandpa is a soul, just like we all are, right? Well, he once had a little baby body which grew older, and then he had a family, and then you came around and you became his grandchild. Well, last week grandpa's body stopped working so he went back to the magic air with all his friends. He is now watching over us and he will always love you."

I realize that the only expert in raising your child is you, the parent. My hope is that this book will spark a sense of recognition and confirmation in both of you, therefore, increasing the amount of trust and love between you and your son or daughter. I was talking with a woman the other day who told me that she was so happy that there was a book on this subject, because now "it wasn't just mom saying it."

Please contact me and let me know your child's responses to the story, any successes you've had with the information, questions you may have, or any assistance you'd like from me. I welcome it all!

All my lovin',
Rich

EPILOGUE

At some point, children might ask the question, "If I am a soul, where do I come from?"

Well, based on all my studies and experiences in this arena, my favorite response has always been:

"Sweetheart, you don't come from anywhere. Everything comes from you."

REFERENCES

Book: Mark Gober – *An End to Upside Down Thinking - Dispelling the Myth That the Brain Produces Consciousness, and the Implications for Everyday Life* - Waterside Press – 2018

Book: Dr. Bruce Greyson M.D. – *After – A Doctor Explores What Near Death Experiences Reveal about Life and Beyond* - St. Martin Publishing Group – 2021

Book: Rich Nisbet – *This Is Not the End Beautiful Friend – Steps to Help Someone at the End-of-Life Maintain Peace and Dignity… While Providing Guidance and Reassurance to Everyone Else* - Robertson Publishing– 2019

Book: Jim B. Tucker M.D. – *Before – Children's Memories of Previous Lives* - St. Martins Publishing Group – 2021

Book: Byron Katie - *Loving What Is – Four Questions That Can Change Your Life –* Harmony - 2001

Instagram - @michael.love444

Podcast: Rich Nisbet - It's The Question - Episode #15 - *The Life Cycle –* https://aboveitall360.com/podcasts/

Audio: *The Coolest Near-Death Experience Ever!* https://aboveitall360.com/story/near-death-experience-tbd/

Song: Rich Nisbet – *We'll Meet Again -* https://open.spotify.com/track/3xQq3Z9aHlKZw0PqOlBkpQ

Contact Rich:
Email: rich@richnisbet.com
Website: richnisbet.com